THE MOST
Beautiful Rose

THE MOST
Beautiful Rose

Memoir Of An Italian Immigrant's
Extraordinary Childhood

DOMENICA CALABRESE

ReadersMagnet, LLC

The Most Beautiful Rose: Memoir Of An Italian Immigrant's Extraordinary Childhood
Copyright © 2020 by Domenica Calabrese. All rights reserved.

Published in the United States of America
ISBN Paperback: 978-1-952896-76-7
ISBN eBook: 978-1-952896-77-4

All rights reserved. No part of this publication may be reproduced, stored in a retrieval system or transmitted in any way by any means, electronic, mechanical, photocopy, recording or otherwise without the prior permission of the author except as provided by USA copyright law.

The opinions expressed by the author are not necessarily those of ReadersMagnet, LLC.

ReadersMagnet, LLC
10620 Treena Street, Suite 230 | San Diego, California, 92131 USA
1.619.354.2643 | www.readersmagnet.com

Book design copyright © 2020 by ReadersMagnet, LLC. All rights reserved.
Cover design by Ericka Obando
Interior design by Shemaryl Tampus

Contents

Dedication vii

Chapter 1.   Birth and Early Years. 1
Chapter 2.   Nonna Vincenza Meets Mussolini 3
Chapter 3.   The Family Grows 4
Chapter 4.   Memories of My Mother 5
Chapter 5.   More Cherished Memories 6
Chapter 6.   Celebrations, Customs, and Traditions. 8
Chapter 7.   The New Village 10
Chapter 8.   Tragedy and Heartbreak 12
Chapter 9.   Aftermath 14
Chapter 10.   The Orphanage 16
Chapter 11.   Emigration to America 18
Chapter 12.   Trip Back Home 20

A Story Worth Sharing. 23
Prologue 29
Epilogue 31
Message to My Children. 33
Vocabulary 35
About the Author 37

Dedication

I dedicate my book to my beloved son Mark Tedeschi
Lost him in 2012 with brain tumor
Always in my heart forever
Young love,
Mom.

In memory of my son-in-law Jeff White and to my beloved parents
Love and miss you very much

CHAPTER 1
Birth and Early Years

It was late morning on May 2, 1949, that I first saw the light of day in a tiny farming village called Pagliarone, in the Italian province of Molise. At that time, my family was comprised of four people: my mother, Leontina Lombardi, my father, Santo Calabrese, my brother, Angelo, and my sister, Maria, who were seven and five years old, respectively.

In those days in Italy, it was customary for children to be named after their paternal grandparents, especially if they were deceased. Since my father's grandmother died before I was born, I bear her name, Domenica.

When I was nine months old, my parents almost lost me. I became ill with pneumonia and went into a coma. My parents were desperate to save me, but there were no doctors in our small village. My *zio* Liberato took a horse and traveled about five miles to find a doctor who could help me. Fortunately, that doctor saved my life.

My father's parents were Michele Calabrese and Marianna Lombardi. His mother died when he was only six. He grew up as an only child, and was raised by his maternal grandmother. By the time my father was in his teens, it was evident that a younger woman was needed in the household. Thus, my parents married young, at age eighteen.

My village consisted of many small *contrade*. At the center was my house, part of a thirteen-family community. In summer, my second-floor balcony was covered with red geraniums and pink, white, and red carnations, cascading down. The beautiful sight and unbelievable aroma attracted all passersby.

Every Sunday, all the townspeople attended Mass in our most beautiful little church, which had marble columns. Everyone in Pagliarone was Roman Catholic. We were all baptized in that church, *La Chiesa Madre*.

The village fountain, bubbling abundant spring water, was an important site in our town. It had anterior and posterior tubs. The front tub was used to allow the animal to quench their thirst before retiring to the barn for the night. The women of the village washed their laundry in the back tub.

Behind the fountain, flowing cleanly and tranquilly, was a tiny brook, on its way to join the larger river, *La Vandra*. Near that spot, my parents owned a small piece of land, in which they cultivated vegetables, figs, plums, grapes, and many flowers, especially roses of all colors. My mom loved flowers! To gain access to the garden, it was necessary to cross the brook. My father situated a piece of wood large enough to reach the other side. Passing under an arch of light pink roses, a small wooden gate, also constructed by my dad, invited us to enter.

Unlike my father who was an only child, my mother came from a family with ten children: Pasquale (who died at eighteen months) Maria Guiseppa, Luciano, Liberato, Malinda, Diletto, my mom Leontina, Adelmo, Angiolina, and Florinda Maria. My maternal grandparents, Salvatore and Vincenza, lived close by. My grandfather was a forester. My grandmother, a deeply religious and intelligent woman, was a midwife. She was the one everyone sought out for sage advice or in time of need, especially when the birth of a child was imminent. The townspeople, having no money, recompensed my *nonna* with fruits and vegetables harvested from their fields.

When World War I broke out, three of my uncles, Luciano, Liberato, and Diletto, were called to serve their country. The youngest, Diletto, was taken prisoner in Africa. It was a most difficult time for my grandmother, Nonna Vincenza. She prayed ardently for their safe return. One fine day, all three of her sons came home safe and sound. Her prayers were answered.

CHAPTER 2

Nonna Vincenza Meets Mussolini

In 1931, my village was hit by a severe landslide, which took with it many houses. Others were badly damaged and rendered unlivable. Subsequently, Mussolini's government reconstructed the village in a more secure place. The government decided to assign the new homes, free of charge, to families in need. My grandmother needed a house, but she was denied by the state of Molise. One day she decided to visit *Il Duce*, Benito Mussolini, personally. She traveled by train and arrived at the Fascist dictator's castle. She was immediately stopped by guards at the gate. Emphatically they declared, "*Signora*, it is impossible to enter the palace without an appointment!" My grandmother told the men to inform Il Duce that there was a woman at the gate who had sacrificed three sons to war, and she needed to speak with him urgently.

The gates were opened and Mussolini himself appeared! He invited my grandmother to join him for lunch. My grandmother shared that she was in desperate need of a house, but the state of Molise had denied her. Benito Mussolini took sympathy upon my grandmother and her story. He told her to go home and she and her family would be given a house. And, indeed, they were. What a brave woman my grandmother was!

My Nonna Vincenza died of cancer in 1954 when I was only five years old. But I still remember her face and her tall, slim figure wearing a long skirt. She wore a bandana on her head and tied it behind her neck. A small sprig of *erba fina* was pinned to her waist. I can still see her walking down the rocky path that would take her to our home to visit with her daughter, my mom.

CHAPTER 3
The Family Grows

WHEN I WAS ALMOST FOUR years old, we welcomed a new baby girl into our family, on February 21, 1953. My mom named her Anna Emerenziana. Her first name was to honor St. Anne, mother of the Virgin Mary, and her middle name was in honor of St. Anne's mother. Anna was a healthy baby and toddler, but when she was five years old, she began experiencing stomach problems. Every time my mom gave her something to eat, she was unable to keep the food down. My parents were devastated and once again, frantic to find a doctor who could help their child. My mom and my sister, Maria, took Anna from town to town in search of a doctor who could cure my younger sister's malady. They finally found one who determined what the problem was, so, thank God, Anna's health improved greatly.

On February 8, 1956, my mom gave birth to another baby girl, my sister Bambina. Her name in Italian literally means "little girl." She was named after my father's aunt. Here in America she was known as "Bam-Bam" when she was young. Eventually, she became known as "Bambi." Now she is a beautician here in Torrington, and everyone knows and swears by the reputation of "Hair by Bambi."

After four girls in a row, my parents finally had another boy. My brother, Salvatore, with blonde, curly locks, was born on October 10, 1958. He was the first child to be born in our new home. However, he was not the last child my parents would have.

???though my mom had lots of mouths to feed, she always managed to share food with those less fortunate than we.

???where did you find me?" (You see, back in the 1950s, especially in Italy, nobody even had the "birds and the bees" discussion, and children believed they were "found" somewhere.) Without hesitating, my mom answered, "One morning, I went in the garden and saw **the most beautiful rose**, wide open. I looked inside and there you were! So, I took you home and now you are mine." In retrospect, I think: How beautiful a mother's words can be, even if they are a little white lie."

CHAPTER 4
Memories of My Mother

My father had relatives who lived here in the United States. Often, they would send us packages from America. What excitement for my siblings and me! Inside were items we couldn't possibly afford ourselves or weren't available in our little town: chocolate kisses, hard candy, crackers, household, and many, various other items. At the bottom of the package we'd find beautiful fabrics, with which my mom made new dresses for her girls. We thought we were little princesses parading around in American outfits!

We were neither rich nor poor. We were just a large family with lots of love, doing the best we could for those times. My parents were well respected in our community and throughout the surrounding towns.

Mom was no doctor, but she was the person the villagers would come to call in their time of need. Like her mother before her, mom was a sought-after midwife. She was one courageous woman. Right next door to our house, door-to-door, lived my best friend, Michelina, her brother, Tonino, her father, Nicola, and Cristina, her young and beautiful mother. Cristina had a heart condition that kept her from living a "normal" life. Often, she was sick during the night Her husband would then knock on the wall that separated their room from my parents' room. That was the signal for my mom to go next door and give Cristina the doctor-ordered needle she needed.

Unfortunately for Cristina, there was no cure. She died at age twenty-six. She left her family and our entire village in deep sorrow. Even so, life went on, the children grew up, but the pain remained in all the hearts of the people she touched.

CHAPTER 5

More Cherished Memories

As a child I enjoyed playing with my friends of the village. We'd love to run in the fields, free as birds. We'd swing on ropes tied to big trees. We would have contests spree who could touch the tree's branches. In spring, the fields were covered with bright, green grass, dotted with blankets of purple violets have such a wonderful aroma, it made you want to take a bath in them. If I close my eyes, I can still see and smell those violets, and the clean air around them.

I also loved my farm. We had pear trees, fig trees and walnut trees. Our field were covered with golden wheat, corn, potatoes, *ceci*, tomatoes, all the Mother Nature had to offer. A brook of clear, spring water babbled nearby. The farmers from my village would come and quench their thirst after a long day's work in the hot sun.

My brother, Angelo, worked the fields with my father, while my sister, Maria, was along helping my mom with the housework. I, too, had to help out, even though I was only six. When I got home from school, I had to do my homework. Then mounted a beautiful, red horse. He was a big, but gentle animal. On each side of him there was a wooden container, the two held together with string. My mom would fill them with *concime*, and off we went to the fields, my horse and I. When we reached our destination, I emptied the container without getting off the horse. My father and my brother would then spread the manure over the fields, filling the dirt with nutrients, hoping for bountiful summer and autumn harvests.

On the way to the fields, far from home, I would travel on rocky, dirt roads, over hills, rivers and forests. Once in a while, a bunny or a fox would peek out of a bush! As a small girl, I was told I had a beautiful singing voice. My singing was my company. As I sang those traditional Italian folk songs I'd heard my family sing over and over, my horse seemed to be listening. And, if I'm not mistaken, I think he enjoyed it, too. With his steady, low gallop, that wonderful, giant animal always brought me home safe.

One late spring day, my brother, Angelo, and I were working in the fields not too far from our home. Suddenly, a violent storm broke out. Lightning flashed, thunder rumbled, and hail pelted us. There was no place for us to take shelter and be safe. I was scared! My brother took me by the hand and, together, we ran as fast as we knew how. Across the River *Vallone* we went. Soon we arrived home soaked from head to toe. Mom greeted us wearing a concerned but relieved look. She took us near the fire and treated us to a delicious dish of *polenta*. On top there was sauce and fresh, homemade cheese, courtesy of our own cows.

One winter day, our town was immobilized by a great big snowstorm. Everything looked beautiful. But the snow was so high that we had to shovel paths to go feed the animals and to get water at the fountain. It was a dire situation. The government had to send helicopters parachuting boxes of food down to the villagers.

One year, my father and my cousin Salvatore, *Zia* Giuseppina's son, went into the forest to make charcoal. This consisted of covering piles of wood with dirt or sod. Then, a fire was built at the bottom of the pile, allowing the wood to burn slowly. They would actually live on the site for approximately one month. On the way home, my father would stop at a store and fill his pockets with candies for us. We were so excited to see him walk through the door, even if he was black from head to toe!

My mom's sister, Angiolina, was married to *Zio* Giovanni and lived in the woods, approximately two miles from my village. They had two children: my cousin, Luciana, who was one year younger than I, and my cousin Salvatore who was two years my junior. My two *cugini* attended school at the village, making the long trip on foot both ways. Often, after school, I would gather my cows, and the three of us would head together to the pastures near their home. The cows ate the healthy, green grass that grew on the hills of our village.

Sometimes, while the cows ruminated, we three would wander down, barefoot, to *La Vandra*, the river that separated the hills from my cousins' home. Luciana and I would pull up our skirts a little so they wouldn't get wet, and Salvatore would pull up his pants. We shrieked with delight as the cold water splashed against our legs! My Zio Giovanni handmade a bamboo trap to catch trout, but the three of us would try to catch the fish with our bare hands. What fun we had in that river! What wonderful memories.

CHAPTER 6
Celebrations, Customs, and Traditions

IN 1958, MY FATHER'S COUSIN'S son, Aurelio, married a beautiful girl from *Isernia*. Her name was Assuntina. She was an accomplished seamstress and sewed clothes for many people. As was customary, there was a big feast that day. My mother with the help of other local women, cooked a big meal for all the out-of-town guests. At night, there was lots of dancing and singing. When the celebration ended, the bridal couple retreated to their second-story room. The rest of us all gathered together under their balcony to serenade the newlyweds. We kept singing until they came to the balcony and acknowledged us. Now, doesn't that tradition make you want to get married in Italy!?!

Near our barn was a big *ara*. Every year we brought onto this field our newly harvested wheat. A huge combine was used to cut and thresh the wheat. Threshing is separating the grain from the straw. Virtually everyone in the village was busy bringing wheat to huge wooden containers we all had behind our houses. Then we would wash the grain and let it dry in the sun. Later, we'd fill up sacks of wheat, place them on either side of our trusty donkeys, and bring them to the *mulino*. Here, it would be ground into flour, from which we made many loaves of bread.

When Easter approached each year, we knew the splendor of spring was upon us. The green grass colored the fields, while the blooming fruit trees sent their scent in the breeze. Each tree covered with flowers was a sight to behold indeed. Potatoes, corn, chickpeas, and many other crops began to grow. It was once again time to work in the fields, after the long, needed rest of winter.

From spring until fall, villagers celebrated many Saints' feast days. If you look at a Roman Catholic calendar, you will note that every day is the feast of some Saint. At night, we could see the fireworks and hear the bands playing from far away.

Every year, in June, in front of my house, all the villagers gathered together to celebrate the Feast of St. Anthony. The kids could hardly contain their excitement! The band regaled us with wonderful music. Then there was a Mass to honor St. Anthony. Following the Mass, the statue of St. Anthony went on parade, with all the townspeople following. Everyone would pin money on his vestments as the procession moved along. The farmers would donate their little lambs to St. Anthony. Those animals would then be sold, and the money made was used to help defray the cost of the feast. At night, singers came to entertain us all.

THE MOST BEAUTIFUL ROSE

My favorite feast of the year always was and always will be *La Notte di Natale*, Christmas Eve. In Italy, Christmas Eve was a very important night. There were abundant foods and the family is together. Little children were everywhere, excited with anticipation. Each child wrote a letter to his or her father and hid it under papa's dinner plate. At the end of the meal, which included our traditional *frittelle*, the children would take their letters, stand on chairs, and read them to everyone. I proudly read my letter, and we all received a few *lire* for our efforts.

Our Christmas tree, usually a *ginepro*, was cut from the nearby woods. It wasn't placed in a stand as we do here in the States, but rather hung, upside down from the kitchen ceiling. The tree was decorated with edibles: apples, oranges, tangerines, chestnuts, *torroni*, and candies –– whatever the family had on hand.

Then it was time for Midnight Mass, the most beautiful Mass of the year for me. Waiting for the birth of Jesus left me in awe. The organ was played by an old man who had no formal musical training, but sounded wonderful just the same. We couldn't wait for him to play the most popular Christmas song of all Italy, "*Tu Scendi Dalle Stelle*," so we could sing along. Yes, Christmas Eve was a beautiful, magical night in our little town.

On the night of January 5th, children would hang their stockings on the chimney in the houses that La Befana would come by and fill them with goodies.

The next morning, all the good little boys and girls would be happy to find oranges, sausages, and maybe even candy. Those who misbehaved, however, could expect to find charcoal, a pig's ear, or a pig's tail in their stocking!

The intent was to teach them a lesson. I never found these items in my stocking, thank God. My brother, Angelo, though, all the time!

The Christmas tree would come down on this day, too, January 6th, the Epiphany. Just as the Christ Child received gifts from the three wise men on this day, so would we. All the good goodies hanging on the tree were taken off and shared by all the members of the family, especially the children.

CHAPTER 7
The New Village

When our village was hit with a horrible mudslide, which badly damaged many houses, we were forced to leave our homes, our barns, and our beloved village and move "uptown." The government had built homes for the neediest. The new village was located about two miles away from the old one. Every morning, we would go back to the village, on foot, to tend to our animals and our fields.

The new village was named *Villa San Michele*. The new house was nice; it had two bedrooms, a kitchen, a dining room, and a bathroom. There was a beautiful church with a big *piazza* in front of it. It seemed to embrace the whole town. There was also a railroad nearby. Often we'd hear the train's roar and its whistle blow.

This new town was an adventure for us. Each morning, a traveling salesman driving a truck, stopped in the middle of the village. With his loudspeaker he would announce what was for sale that day: fruit, cloth, shoes, kitchen utensils, and other household items. The next day, perhaps different things would be for sale. We'd rush over to see the merchandise up close.

For the kids from our small village of Pagliarone, life in Villa San Michele was quite different. Even the people seemed different. Some of them owned a radio, some owned a car! Everything was probably better there but, for us, it was a joy to go back to our old village every morning… back to the routine of tending our

Domenica's grandfather and her siblings

Me when I was 15 years old and the last years in Italy

animals and our fields. It was here, in our new house, in the new village, that my mom gave birth to our new brother, Salvatore, in October 1958.

CHAPTER 8
Tragedy and Heartbreak

In October 1959, my aunt Angiolina and her family left our hometown to go live in Toronto, Canada. Her brothers Adelmo and Liberato, and her sister Maria, already lived there. My cousins Luciana and Salvatore would have to leave me.

The day of the departure, they stayed in my house with my mom for the last time. The rented bus arrived, ready to take the family to the port of Naples. There they would board a ship that would take them across the Atlantic to Halifax. Family members wanted to go along to say good-bye. My mom was expecting again, with the baby due in a few weeks, so she was unable to accompany them.

I remember the pain in my mom's and my aunt's eyes when they embraced and said *arrivederci*. They were very close, as close as two sisters can be. My aunt told my mom, "As soon as I get a job, I will send for you and the family." Everyone boarded and the bus disappeared in the distance.

My mom was near the fireplace stirring the fire, crying silently. I sat in a small chair and pulled up next to her. I put my head on her lap, as tears streamed down my own face. With her warm hand she stroked my hair. "Don't cry," she said. "You will see your cousins again." It was a very sad day for me. Days, then weeks went by. Finally, we received a letter stating that the voyage went well and that my aunt and her family had reached their destination safely.

Every day I went down to the old village to do my chores. I took a group of cows to the pasture near my cousins' house. Yes, the house was still there, but now it was empty, abandoned. Everything was silent. Quietly, I began to cry. I looked up at the clear, blue sky, dotted with clouds that looked like giant cotton balls enjoying the sun. I wondered why they seemed so happy when I was so miserable. I called my cousins' names. No answer. No more running up and down the river, barefoot. No more trout trap. Just an abandoned house surrounded by vineyards and fruit and nut trees: peaches, plums, cherries, figs, olives, chestnuts, walnuts, and hazelnuts. And, since no one lived there now, any passersby could just help themselves.

On November 6, 1959, one month after my aunt arrived in Toronto, my mom gave birth to her last child, Michelino. We wrote my aunt the news and said everything was okay. We were all very happy to have a new little brother. My brother, Salvatore, was only one year old when our youngest brother was born. My sister, Maria, was only fourteen, but she took excellent care of my mom and the baby. I, too, at ten years of age, helped in the best way I knew how. I brought soup to my mom in bed so she could get strong. The doctor had said that since this was her seventh delivery, it would take her some time to recuperate.

One day, when I brought her food, I realized my mom wasn't herself. I spoke to her, but she did not respond. She just looked at me with fear in her eyes, unable to speak. Crying, I ran down the stairs calling for my sister. My father got word to a friend from a nearby town to come quickly with his car. They would bring my mom to a hospital in *Agnone*.

My mom needed help to get into and to sit down in the automobile. I was devastated to see her go. I grabbed the car door handle and frame and sobbed loudly enough to get my mom's attention. She looked back at me, but her eyes were like crystal, not blinking, just staring at me. I called her name, still weeping. People pulled me off the car, and down the dirt road they went, my father, my sister, *zia* Maria Lucia, and my mom… left behind were the townspeople, the other children, and I, desolate and confused.

When they finally arrived at the hospital, my mom was taken immediately to the Emergency Room. My father and aunt went in with her, but my sister was not allowed to since she was a minor. She was left to wait alone for some news to come regarding our mother. Two nurses were talking, unaware of my sister. One said to the other, "Poor woman… they waited until she was on her deathbed before they brought her to the hospital."

Hearing this exchange, Maria burst into tears. The nurses then tried to calm her down and asked her, "What's wrong? Why are you crying?" My sister sobbed, "That is my mother you were talking about!" The nurses reassured my sister that since mom was now here in the hospital, she was going to be fine.

Night fell. My father and my sister came home, but my aunt stayed at the hospital to help my mom. My cousin, Amelina, also took turns relieving my father and my aunt at my mom's side. After a few days, my mother felt a little better. Already she began to worry: How was the new baby doing? How was my father going to plant the crops all alone? How were the other children managing? Zia Maria Lucia assured her that he had enough help and that everything else was okay. "You just concentrate on getting well so we can go home," my aunt told her. Sadly, that would not be the case. My mom passed away at 3:00 a.m. on November 25, 1959.

We did not find out, however, since there were no telephones. That morning, my father and my cousin, Amelina, got up very early. Their intention was to catch a bus to go visit my mom. In the distance, they spotted car lights piercing the darkness. My father and my cousin decided to wait and ask the driver for a ride to the bus station. When the automobile got near them, it came to a stop, right in front of our house. What my father heard next were shocking and unbelievable words. The driver informed him that my mother was in the car. However, she wasn't sitting up or talking… My aunt was holding my mother's lifeless body across her lap.

A painful, deafening cry awoke the townspeople and us. Everyone came rushing out of his or her house. No one knew what was going on, but they could tell that it was not good. I remember my brothers and sisters and I running outside, looking at our mom, who was no longer looking at us.

CHAPTER 9

Aftermath

Some people tried to console my father, but he was broken and weary. They helped him inside the house. Others placed my mom on the table. She was wrapped in a white sheet. My father was in deep, unspeakable sorrow. The only words he seemed to utter were, "It's so dark in my house," even though some lights were on. I ran to the table to see my mom, tears flooding my ten-year-old face. I was incredulous that she had left us. I touched her and she was still warm. I called her name many times, begging her to open her eyes and say "Don't cry… I will be fine." But such words she did not speak… no words at all. My mom was gone… really gone… forever.

Some ladies took my mom to her room. They dressed her in a lovely, grey suit, which my Zia Angiolina had given her before she left for Canada. Assuntina had sewn the outfit for my aunt. My mom was a pretty woman with long, black hair. Every morning before she started her day of chores and taking care of all her children, she would brush that beautiful hair and tie it back in braids or in a bun. I am the only one of her seven children to inherit her long, black hair, which she would comb into braids for me. Now my mom was gone. She was only thirty-seven years old.

My mom was a woman with a very busy life. But she was always ready and happy to help others. She loved nature. She loved God, the Virgin Mary, and all the Saints. And she loved us. After her death, all the townspeople came to pay their respects to a woman who had always been there for them. My town lost a great lady that day. Her name is still alive on the lips and in the hearts of all those who knew her.

For us, it was a most dreadful loss. Our daunting task was to get adjusted to a home without its most important person of all: a mother. We had to learn to do things ourselves. No more of mom's hugs. When we scraped our knees or when we were sick in bed, we kids were left with only the memories in our hearts of our wonderful mother. It was so hard not to be able to call the most beautiful name: Mamma.

With the help of our family and friends, we were able to make it, little by little, one day at a time. My one-year-old brother, Salvatore, would walk around the house, his arms opened wide, calling mom's name. My sister, Maria, was convinced that mom was right there, hugging her little boy.

Night was the worst of all. Everyone would go to bed except my father. He would sit alone, near the fireplace, crying. He was crying for the loss of his beloved wife, a woman who had given him seven children, and whose life was cruelly cut short, as was their time together. Never again could he buy her a new dress or say thank you for all she'd done.

At night, I would pretend to go to bed. But, then I would sneak down the stairs and sit on one step, undetected by my father. I was crying, too, keeping him company in his sorrow.

We displayed on our kitchen wall an enlarged photo of my mom in her wedding dress. A light beneath it burned twenty-four hours a day. Though life went on, the wound in our hearts remained fresh, and lingers there to this day for all of us.

CHAPTER 10
The Orphanage

My father found a government job in conservation, my brother, Angelo, worked the fields, and my sister, Maria, was raising the children and being our mom. After school I went down to the village to take care of the animals, and then back home at nightfall. It was now 1960, and a few months had passed since my mom's death.

One day, Don Edolo, a local priest and a friend of my parents, came by to visit my father. Don Edolo told my father that he was running an orphanage in *Castel di Sangro*. The priest tried to convince my father that the best thing to do was to send me there. The orphanage would take care of my schooling, my clothing, and my meals. I would get a higher education and learn a trade for the future. All this, gratis.

My father was not at all happy to see his child leave home, but in time, he realized it made sense for me to go. My father, my sister, Maria, and I caught a train whose destination was the orphanage. The first stop was at the hairdresser. My beautiful long braids had to be cut off. There wasn't even anyone available to take my picture before those cruel scissors began to shear my locks. I cried when I saw my face looking like a tomboy and at my hair in the garbage pail.

When we met the other orphans, they were all very curious to see a new student among them. They were all over me trying to make me feel at home. My friend, Michelina, was there, too. She'd been there for two years. She was very happy to see me. We even had our beds next to each other. Though I was happy to see her, too, my mind was back home with my family. When my father and my sister had to leave, it was a very emotional separation. That night was very sad for me. I cried myself to sleep.

I started school the day after I arrived. Every week, they would call and tell me that there was a gentleman waiting for me in the hallway. It was my father, bringing with him foods I used to love to eat at home: farm-fresh eggs, homemade sausage, and homemade bread. Afterwards, I would share the goodies with my best friend. A year later, my sister, Anna, came to join me. It was a happy time for me since someone from my family was with me.

In 1962, we received word that our sister, Maria, was to marry a boy in town named Giovanni. He worked at the railroad station. The wedding was set for January. I was halfway through my schooling when I was told I'd have to leave the orphanage to go take care of my little brothers and sister. My sister, Anna, would remain, however. My going back home spelled the end of becoming a hairdresser.

The wedding day came. As was customary, my sister went to live with her new inlaws, up the street from our house. I was nearly thirteen years old didn't look the same as I did when I left Villa San Michele for the orphanage I had matured, and the boys in town noticed. Some of them expressed on interest in me.

Often at night, there was a dance. I loved to dance! But, my father didn't like the idea of my going dancing. Sometimes I'd sneak out with an older cousin, and prayed all night that I wouldn't get caught.

There was a woman in town who had a small store. She was holding a raffle for several prizes. There were many, but among the best were a gorgeous doll and colossal chocolate Easter egg, the latter having a special prize inside. I really wanted that doll. I sold eggs so I could get tickets. My cousin came running down to me on the day of the drawing. I had won the gigantic Easter egg, he informed me. Well, it wasn't my first choice, but it was beautiful. It was wrapped in multi-colored, lustrous paper, and was tied with a pretty blue ribbon. It was the biggest egg I had ever seen!

In January 1964, my nephew, Edmondo, was born. When spring came, my sister and I took the children for a walk to a pine grove. We had heard that doctors believed breathing in the pine air was healthy for you and would clean your lungs. One day, a truck carrying fruit drove by. We soon noticed that a case of beautiful peaches was on the ground. What fun we all had feasting on those luscious fruits that had fallen off the truck!

CHAPTER 11
Emigration to America

THE SAME YEAR EDMONDO WAS born, my father remarried. He married Maria, a woman we all knew, who already lived in America. That way, my father could take all his minor children, Michelino, Salvatore, Bambina, Anna, and me, age five to fifteen, to a new land to live a better life.

It was in February 1965, that we left Villa San Michele to embark on a journey to the unknown. Again, the entire town came to say *arrivederci*. With tear-stained faces, friends and family wished us the best of luck in the new land. My own friends were crying, "Come back if you can… we will wait for you… we will never forget you buona fortuna." We'd all grown up together and had been companions for nearly fifteen years.

My two elder siblings, Maria and Angelo, accompanied us to Fiumicino Airport in Rome. Just two days before, Edmondo had turned one-year-old. Now we were leaving him. We hugged over and over, each of us in pain, finding it very difficult to let go. Saying good-bye and leaving each other was the second-hardest event my family had to face.

My seat was near a window. Through that small glass circle, I could see my sister and my brother waving and wiping their eyes. I reached in my pocket and took out a white handkerchief. I waved to them with it, hoping that they would see me. The plane took off against clear, blue skies, allowing us an awesome view of our

Reunited with my cousins here at the USA

My aunt Angelina and I

THE MOST BEAUTIFUL ROSE

beautiful Rome we were leaving behind: palm trees, golden roofs, breathtaking fountains, beautiful sunshine, no coats needed.

Eight hours later we landed in New York City. A big snowstorm greeted us. We needed to deplane and take a connecting flight to Bradley Field Airport. The Alitalia pilot took my little brothers, Michael and Salvatore in his arms and took us to the other airplane in time for us to board. After a much shorter flight, we landed in Windsor Locks, Connecticut. When we got off the plane, we were horrified to see that no one was there to meet us!

Someone helped my father find the phone number and dialed Zia Angiolina. She and her family had moved from Toronto to Torrington, Connecticut. They now lived with her father-in-law, Luciano, and her sister-in-law Eva and their families. My aunt said that because of the storm, our relatives who were picking us up were running late. But, she reassured him that they would be at the airport very soon. Not long after that, they were there to meet us. They brought three cars!

We were to live in a house my aunt Angiolina had rented for us. It was located just two streets below where she lived. When we got to our new house, I was reunited with my dear cousins, Luciana and Salvatore. It was wonderful to see them again, but it wasn't the same. More than five years had gone by since we last saw each other. They looked different, they were no longer little kids. They spoke English. They had American cousins they were close with, Maria Grazia (Mary) and Anna Lucia (Annie.) They had new friends. Sometimes they would take me with them and their companions, but I felt lonely and out-of-place. I missed my home and my friends. I cried every day and I wanted to go home. I visited my aunt Angiolina often; she was my best company.

Since I wasn't sixteen years old yet, I was required by law to go to school. But, because I didn't speak English, they placed me in filth grade! You see, in 1965, there was no such thing as E.S.L (English as a Second Language Education. Imagine: There I was, a fully developed young woman, stuck among ten-year-olds! And I didn't understand a word of what teacher and the students were saying. It was sheer boredom and humiliation!

On May 2, 1965, sixteenth birthday, I quit school. Soon after, I met a girl named Carmela, her sister, Violanda, and their parents, Carolina and Giuseppd. They bestfriended me, and through Carmela, I found my first paying job. I worked at Hitchcock Chair Company in Riverton, Connecticut, caning and rushing chairs. I was the youngest person in the entire factory. There I met another girl, Filomena. We became very close friends, and later then, she asked me to be her son, Paul's, Godmother.

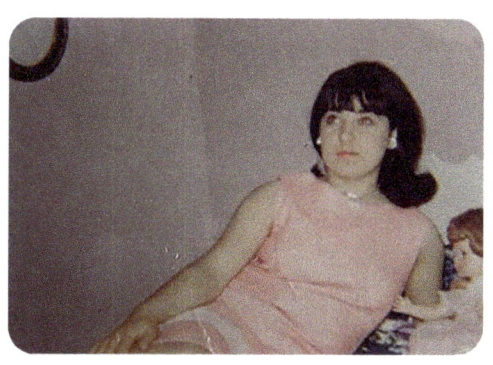

Sweet sixteenth in America

Still, my days were lonely, and I felt homesick. I spent most of my weekend in my room listening to Italian songs played on an old record player someone had given me. I wrote letters to my sister in Italy and told her all about America. I also wrote to a boy who had put a ring on my finger when I was fifteen, promising that I would go back someday and we would be married but it never happens. The mailman was my best friend. He knew what I wanted him to bring me. Every time he had a letter for me, he'd call out loud, "Look! I've got a letter from Italy!"

CHAPTER 12
Trip Back Home

IN 1967, MY SISTER GAVE birth to my niece, Leondina, the first granddaughter to be named after my mother. My brother, Angelo, joined the family by coming to America. Soon, we began planning a trip back home. We'd go in November 1967. It would be two years and a half that I'd been away from my homeland. I was counting the days, the hours, the minutes, until the time arrived for us to depart. That morning, Torrington again was hit by a big snowstorm. Our plane was delayed. Back home, my sister and my mom's father, *Nonno* Salvatore, who was bedridden from having suffered a stroke, were very worried about us. Finally, the plane took off.

Halfway through the flight, the sun was shining brightly. We were excited! Soon the pilot announced that we were approaching Rome. I looked out the window. My body froze with emotion. The city looked as beautiful as I remembered it. My sister and my brother-in-law were there to meet us. After hugs and greetings, we picked up our luggage and found our way to Giovanni's car. As we drove away, I knew that in a few hours, I would see my beloved hometown again.

As we were getting close, I asked my brother-in-law to please stop the car. I got out and stood on a small hill. I looked down, and there it was my village. The houses were still standing, but no one was living in them. There was the little road I walked every day. The fields, uncultivated now, were still there. Tears of joy streamed down my face.

The next stop was the town cemetery. My mom's tomb was still the way we'd left it. Her beautiful photo, ensconced in a protective oval on the marble headstone, looked back at us. And, the little light was still flickering, twenty-four hours a day. Tears of heartbreak streamed down my face.

Back home, my friends were anxiously waiting to see me. We looked at each other like I never left. What a joyous reunion it was! "You look so pretty!" they exclaimed. "You haven't changed --- just got a little older." I looked around, thinking I must be dreaming. And, if so, I hope I never wake up.

After "catching up" with my friends, it was time to eat. I was so looking forward to going down to my old village, that I couldn't wait to finish my dinner. We made our way down the dirt road. When we arrived, I drank in the view. The houses were still standing but were not livable. The *fontana* was in relatively good condition, projecting cold spring water, as always. The old farmers, my friends, were happy to see me again. They were full of questions about America, land of opportunity. The fig trees, and all the other fruit trees, were still thriving and producing annually, fruits for everyone to enjoy.

As *Natale* drew near, the *paesani* were all busy making the traditional fried dough with sugar on top. The hustle-bustle of the season was evident all over town. Then came the usual Christmas Eve dinner, followed by Midnight Mass, to welcome baby Jesus among us.

The church looked magnificent, decorated in full glory. *Il Presepio* boasted a life-size Virgin Mary, St. Joseph, baby Jesus, shepherds, wise men, camels, donkeys, cows, and sheep. Angels and stars hung from above. The High Mass was a beautiful celebration to honor Jesus, who saved mankind. Above us, the church bells were ringing, music to my ears. Soon we were all standing, fervently singing *"Tu Scendi Dalle Stelle."* In my heart I thought, you **can** go home again.

A Story Worth Sharing

Not so long ago, I was visiting my sister, Maria, in Italy, and she recounted this. One morning, a few months after my mom died, my father was in the village to feed the animals. It was winter, so there was lots of snow on the ground. He looked at our garden. A spot of pink color on the rose arch intrigued him. He got closer and discovered a tiny pink rose, fresh as a summer's day, under the blanket of snow. It was the only one there.

My father picked the pretty flower and brought it home. He placed in front of my mom's picture. That rose refused to die. My father took it to the cemetery. When my sister visited my mom's grave, the rose was nowhere to be found. I truly believe my mom never left us. She gave us a pink rose, the color of a mother's love for her children.

I planted that same species of rose in my garden in Torrington. In the first year, a tiny branch remained alive into December. Presently, it blooms beautifully each year, with its pink flowers and sweet scent bringing loving memories of my mother.

During on trip back to Italy, I returned to The Orphanage, but found it abandoned. My room was behind the third window on the left, 2nd floor.

As I sit on the actual fountain wall, memories of days gone by, and experiences we lived, flood my mind. Even though it is virtually abandoned, the spring waters flow abundantly. Behind me is the piece of property my parents owned. The sole survivor is our hazelnut tree. (1980)

Family picture of Mark's wedding day
From right to left; My son Domenic, daughter Tina, Domenica, my beloved son Mark, his wife Erin, my husband Mario, oldest daughter Maria and her beloved husband Jeff.

For my father's 80th birthday, all his children were reunited for the celebration. From left to right, Angelo Calabrese, Maria Calabrese Lombardi, Domenica Calabrese Tedeschi, Anna Calabrese Amoroso, Bambina Calabrese Iannacito, Salvatore Calabrese, and Michael Calabrese in the USA.

A sample of some of the paintings I have recently completed:

Mark & Erin's Backyard in Spring
By Domenica C.

Serenity at Elizabeth Park
West Hartford, Connecticut
By Domenica C.

Farm Girls
By Domenica C.

Prologue

In conversing with the many people I've met over the years, here in the United States, the subject of my childhood invariably comes up. When people hear the circumstances, they are sympathetic, fascinated, and amazed. Repeatedly, I've been told, **"You should write a book!"** I've thought about their words from time to time. And, after much consideration, I decided: Maybe I should. So, here it is, the true story of my childhood.

Epilogue

I HOPE MY MEMOIR WILL INSPIRE all its readers. And, it is my fervent wish that this true story would give orphan children hope, and that it will help them realize that **life will go on…**

Message to My Children

I WANT TO TELL YOU HOW much I appreciate you being my children. I want to thank you for the love you have for me and for appreciating what I have done and do for you. I love you all more than you can imagine. A mother's heart is always the most honest. You are my life and always will be. Remember that life is not always a bed of roses. Roses may be the most beautiful flowers on Earth, but they have thorns.

**All my love,
Mom**

Daughter Tina with her husband Mark

Vocabulary

Agnone- the nearest city that had a hospital
Ara- field; are, in surface measure
Arrivederci- we'll see each other again; good-bye
Buona fortuna- goodluck; good fortune to you
Castel di Sangro- city where the orphanage was located
Ceci- chickpeas; we'd eat them fresh, right out of the pod
Concime- manure we'd spread on our fields
Contrade- sections within a town
Cugina, cugini, cugino- female cousin, (plural) cousins, male cousin
Erba fina- an aromatic herb or grass
Fontana- fountain, a very important site in our village
Frittelle- fritter; fried dough, a tradition at Christmas time
Ginepro- juniper; evergreen used for Christmas trees
Il Duce- The Leader; title by which Benito Mussolini was known
Il Presepio- the Nativity Scene; Crèche
Isernia – a province in southern Italy
La Befana- the good "witch" who put gifts in children's stockings on 1-6
La Chiesa Madre- The Mother Church
La Notte di Natale- Christmas Eve night
La Vandra- river that separated grazing fields from cousins' house
Lire- smallest unit of money; cents
Mamma- mom, mommy, mother
Molino- mill; watermill
Nonna, nonno- grandmother, -father; very important in Italian families
Paesani- fellow countrymen; people from the same town as you
Pagliarone- our original hometown; literally, large straw barn
Piazza- the town square; clearing
Polenta- corn meal, usually served with sauce on top
Signora- lady; madam; wife; Mrs.
Torroni- nougat candies, rectangular prism in shape

"Tu Scendi Dalle Stelle" – literally, You Descend From the Stars; traditional song sung at Midnight Mass; perhaps you've heard it sung in St. Peter Church, in Torrington, CT
Vallone- small river in Pagliarone, author's birthplace
Zia, zio- aunt, uncle; capitalized if person's name follows

About the Author

Domenica Calabrese Tedeschi was born in a small village in the Molise section of Italy. She immigrated to the United States in 1965, at the age of 15, with her father and four of her six siblings. She currently works at the family business, Tedeschi Tile and Marble, in Torrington, CT. Outside of work, she keeps busy cooking delicious Italian meals for her family and friends, and babysitting for her grandchildren. She can also be found in her Art Studio painting flowers, children, landscapes, and locales in rural Italy. Like her mother and grandmother before her, Domenica is very religious and prays the Holy Rosary daily. She is also passionate about writing stories.

The Most Beautiful Rose is her first book. Domenica makes her home in Torrington, CT, with her family.

My grandkids, starting from your right; Joseph, Lorenzo, Caterina & Luca

www.ingramcontent.com/pod-product-compliance
Lightning Source LLC
LaVergne TN
LVHW070218080526
838202LV00067B/6848